Mommy
Tell me about
Haiti

Written by Jeanine Agnant and Alexandra Barbot
Illustrated by Alexandra Barbot

Mommy, tell me about Haiti / Manmi, rakonte m Ayiti
Author: Jeanine Agnant and Alexandra Barbot
Illustration: Alexandra Barbot
Cover design and page layout: Nathalie Jn Baptiste
© Copyright 2009, ABarbot Art

For information, please contact:

Haitian American Historical Society
ABarbot Art
P.O. Box 310085
Miami, FL 33231-0085
Phone : 786-621-0035
Email : haitianhistory@att.net, alexandra@alexandrabarbotart.com
www.haitianhistory.org
www.alexandrabarbotart.com

ISBN 13: 978-1-58432-466-9
ISBN 10: 1-58432-466-X

Dedication

I want to dedicate this book to my grandchildren, and thank the person who helped me publish this book.

Jeanine Agnant

To

The Honorable Dana St.Claire

Partageons i' histoire
de mon Pays Haïti)
un petit pays avec
une grande histoire

Alexandra Joutt
2/22/2017

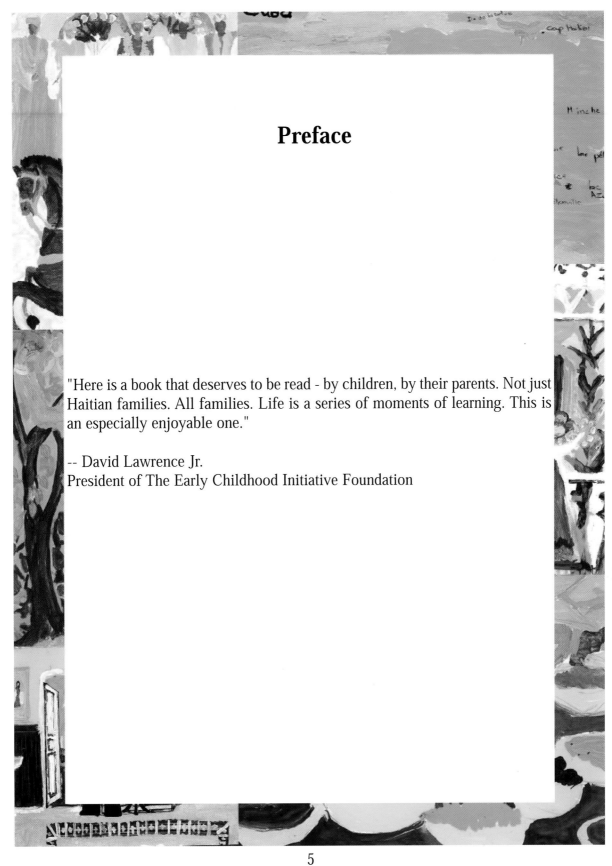

Preface

"Here is a book that deserves to be read - by children, by their parents. Not just Haitian families. All families. Life is a series of moments of learning. This is an especially enjoyable one."

-- David Lawrence Jr.
President of The Early Childhood Initiative Foundation

Very special thanks to:

Commissioner Dennis C Moss
Chairman Miami Dade County Commissions - District 9

Commissioner Audrey M. Edmonson
Miami Dade County - District 3

Commissioner Robert Siedlecki
Commissioner SSFCTP

Major Joseph Bernadel
Co-founder, Toussaint Louverture Highschool for Art and Social Justice

M. David Lawrence
President, Early Childhood Initiative Foundation

Dr. Rudolph Moise
President, Comprehensive Health Center

Andre Lapierre Pardo, PhD
Thespian; President-founder of the **Bob Lapierre Theatre Company, Inc.**

Professor Jean Claude Exulien
First Vice Chair, Haitian American Historical Society

Professor Claude Charles
Second Vice Chair, Haitian American Historical Society

About the illustrator and author

Alexandra Barbot is an illustrator a visual artist and an author. She has a degree from the State University of Port-au-Prince Haiti for law, and a certificate in German language from the Ludwig Maximilian University in Munich, Germany. As an author she published in 1993 "De la protection de l'environement en Haïti" for her master degree in law that will be available in 2011 to the public. She co-published in 1998 an article with two German attorneys "Die wirtshaflichen auswirkungen und die Bekampfung von Produkt piraterie in Deutschland und anderen Landern" in the "le courier du club" for the French and German business club. She co-published and illustrated in 2008 and 2009 with Mrs. Jeanine Agnant "Mommy, tell me about Haiti" and "Tell me about Haiti". She studied art with the internationally renowned Haitian Roland Dorcely. Mrs. Barbot has exhibited her work in Haiti, Germany and France, and has worked with many Haitian and American nonprofit organizations in Miami. She donates her artwork to worthy causes for fund-raising events.

Chapter one

The story of the island

Sitting with their grandmother in the patio, the children were looking forward to story time. Their grandma either would read them a book or tell them a story.

Josephine the youngest one wanted to hear something new today something about the country where her grandma came from.
She asked:

"Mommy, tell me about Haiti?"

"Children, gather around me, and let me tell you the story of my place in the sun. A story so beautiful, you would think that it is a legend, you would not believe it to be true, but it is. Call your brother and listen carefully, I will tell you how sweet life was there when I was growing up."

"Long ago in Haiti lived the native queen of one of the island kingdoms. Her name was Anacaona She was from the Arawak tribe, and her people were peace loving. They liked poetry, dance and music, and they had a religion of their own.

"In a neighboring kingdom lived King Caonabo. The king and the queen had a beautiful wedding and united their territories. They where the first Haitians"

"Were they happy islanders?"

"Yes until Christopher Columbus came and his followers forced the Arawaks to work hard for the gold the island had."

"What did the king and queen do ?"
They fought back, but could not prevent the massacre caused by Colon's partisans.

"What happened then?"
"People from Africa were brought in to replace the first Haitans."

"What happened to the Africans?
Did they survive the hard work?"

"They resisted against the bad treatments of the Europeans. Some of them escaped towards the mountains and revolted often. Then came a great diplomat, the great grand-son of King Gaou Ginou, Great Chief of the Arada tribe in Dahomey, Africa. He was born in Saint-Domingue and was a very thin and smart man. He was called Toussaint Louverture, because, they say, he opened the door to African freedom in the American continent.."

11

"Who was Toussaint Louverture ?"
"He was the one that fought the first great war for Haiti's freedom. He said "No more slaves, we want Haiti free," he had even planned after Haiti was free to go to Dahomey, his grandfather's kingdom in West Africa, to fight the slave trade from there" He started his military career as "aide the Camp" or assistant to General George Biassou

"Did Toussaint Louverture succeed?"

"He was very successful, because in his time, a slave was to be nothing else but a slave. Toussaint,who started his military carrer by being aide de camp for General George Biassou, instead rose to becoming the Governor General of the whole island. He was betrayed and captured by the French, but others after him did succeed, like Jean Jacques Dessalines the Great, Capois Lamort, Alexandre Pétion, and Henri Christophe who became king and built the Citadel Laferière and the 365 doors Palace, "Palais Sans-Souci," near Cap-Haitian, in the northen side of Haïti."

"The first Haitian flag was red and blue. It was sawn together by a lady named
Catherine Flon in the city of Arcahaie where your grandma was born."

"Few people know that the Haitian soldiers were sent to countries in Latin America to help end slavery and bring freedom. And a group of Haitian soldiers, "Les Chasseurs Volontaires de St. Domingue"fought at the Savannah battle in the American Revolution."

"To let people from all over the world know about the great deeds of the young nation, an organization called "Haitian American Historical Society," with the help of the City of Savannah, built a monument to the soldiers. The statue of the little drummer boy in the monument represents the future King Henri Christophe."

Chapter two

Growing up in my island

The children listened to their grandma, then said:
"Oh that is exciting tell us more. What was it like growing up in Haiti?"

"In the summer season we would go to the beach. The sand is the finest and it offers a variety of shades from pink shells in the beaches of Labadie and Cyvadie. And the sumptuous sand of la Jacmelienne beach shines like diamonds."
"Along the coast, we would see the colorful fishing boats in the sea and the women in the fish-market offering freshly caught fish."

"We would go in the plains to the countryside and pick mangos at the farms, or swim amidst the beautiful waterfalls and springs. I swam in Basin Zim, near a city called Hinche, a place with the freshest water."

"The hardworking country people are kind; they plant their crops after the full moon, just like their ancestors did back in Africa."

"In Kenscoff, a place in the mountains where we vacationed in the hot months of the year, I remember country vendors, with their baskets full of goods on their heads, gracefully walking on the road."

"Most of the population, in the countryside are farmers. Sometimes all the men gathered to work on one field known as "Koumbite" and then go on to work on the next field and so on until the lands owned by all the farmers were planted. The women bring the harvest to the market."

"Many children in the countryside did not go to school, but stayed home with their parents. The fortunate ones to go to school, are very proud about it and work hard to get good grades.

I only have good memories of my childhood in Haiti. During the school year, I would go to a school that was led by nuns, and we would play jacks and marbles as well as jump rope or with a hoop."

"In the afternoon, we would walk to my grandma's house where my mom and dad picked me and my four sisters up."

"You were lucky to go to your grandma's house every day."

"We sure were, all my grandma's sisters lived in the same house, every afternoon we were welcomed by the good smells of pain patate, flan, crème brûlée, millefeuille and cake."

"Nobody made 'griot' like my grandma, and aunt Emily made and incredible "lambi". One day, Great Grand Aunt Georgina even made me a crocquembouche."

"Aunt Batilde was the piano teacher. You had better watch your fingers if you played a wrong note. Some days, we would walk to the folkdance course where we were taught the dances brought from Africa."

"The best part about my grandma's house was that at carnival time, all the floats passed by right in front of her house; we enjoyed all the beautiful costumes, ate delicious banana fritters, and danced to the happy tunes of the passing bands."

"That's enough for today, but you can ask your older brother Paul, we often went with him on vacation, which is something he enjoyed very much."

"Paul tell me more about Haiti please, please, pretty please with sugar on top"

" I have a better idea, Josephine, " said Paul
"Why don't we put all that Mommy told us in a book so that more children can learn about Haiti"

"Let's do it ," said Josephine.

More facts for the readers

The Haitian revolution had a major impact for the United States of America : The "Louisiana purchase of April 30th 1803 where the United States bought the lands from the Mississippi to the west of the Rocky Mountain and from New Orleans north to Canada happened because of the Slave Rebellion in St Domingue nowadays Haiti. With the revolt and rebellion against France, Napoleon Bonaparte needed money to pay for the war against Britain and sold all of Louisiana (2,071,840 sq km) for the price of $15,000,000.

In the following pages you will find more information about the "Island of Haiti" before Christopher Columbus landed and after it was freed from slavery by slaves of African descent. You also will find more facts about **"Les Chasseurs-Volontaires de Saint Domingue"** who sailed from Saint Domingue (modern **Haiti**). They were soldiers of African descent who left their families to participate in the Georgia Campaign under French Commander Charles Henri d'Estaing. You also will find information about the **"Haitian American Historical Society"** that built the monument to honor the memory of **"Les Chasseurs Volontaires de St. Domingue"** in **Savannah, Georgia.**

Map of Hispaniola in1492

When Christopher Columbus landed, the island was called Haiti, meaning "land of high mountains" or Quisqueya meaning "mother of the earth" or Bohio in the Arawak language.

Before the first foreigners arrived the island was divided into five kingdoms. The Cacica of Higuey ruled by
Cotubanama; the Cacica of Xaragua ruled by Bohecio whose sister was the famous Anacaona; the Cacica of Magua ruled by Guarionex; the Cacica of Maguana ruled by Caonabo, and the Cacica of Marien ruled by Guacanaguaric..

Map of Haiti

The Spanish called the island Hispaniola, then Santo Domingo. The French called it St. Domingue and after the revolution, Jean Jacques Dessalines called it Haiti, the name chosen by the island's first inhabitants.

27

Haitian Memorial Monument in Savannah

In its fourth year the American Revolution had become an international conflict. Rebelling American colonies and their French allies attempted to capture Savannah from the British in 1779. Haitian soldiers of African descent were part of the allied forces. Following the battle, many of these Haitians were diverted to other military duties, returning to their homes years later, if at all. Several veterans of the campaign became leaders of the movement that made Haiti the second nation in the Western Hemisphere to throw off the yoke of European colonialism.

The largest unit of soldiers of African descent who fought in the American Revolution was the brave "Les chasseurs volontaires de Saint Domingue" from Haiti. This regiment consisted of free men who volunteered for a campaign to capture Savannah from the British in 1779. Their sacrifice reminds us that men of African descent were also present on many other battlefields during the revolution.

n the fall of 1779, over 545 "Chasseurs volontaires" sailed from Saint Domingue, the modern island of Haiti, soldiers of African descent , "Les chasseurs volontaires de Saint Domingue" left their families to participate in the Georgia campaign under French commander Charles Henri d'Estaing.

In the battle of Savannah on October 9, 1779 "Les chasseurs volontaires de Saint Domingues," our forefathers, fought alongside the American army of General Benjamin Lincoln, distinguishing themselves by their bravery. As part of the reserve, they provided cover during the retreat of American and French allies, saving many lives by deterring a fierce counterattack of defending British troops.

Although hundreds of other "Chasseurs volontaires" remain unknown today , a number of them are documented and listed below
PIERRE ASTREL, LOUIS JACQUES BEAUVAIS, JEAN-BAPTISTE MARS BELLEY, MARTIAL BESSE , GUILLAUME BLECK, PIERRE CANGE, JEAN-BAPTISTE CHAVANNES, HENRI CHRISTOPHE, PIERRE FAUBERT, LAURENT FEROU, JEAN-LOUIS FROUMENTAINE, BARTHELEMY-MEDOR ICARD, GEDEON JOURDAN, JEAN PIERRE LAMBERT, JEAN-BAPTISTE LEVEILLE, CHRISTOPHE MORNET, PIERRE OBAS, LUC-VINCENT OLIVER, PIERRE PINCHINAT, JEAN PIVERGER, ANDRE RIGAUD, CESAIRE SAVARY, PIERRE TESSIER, JEROME THOBY, JEAN-LOUIS VILLATE

WE HONOR ALL OF THEIR COLLECTIVE SACRIFICES KNOWN AND UNKNOWN

The drummer represent young Henri Christophe, who participated in the October 9, 1779 Battle of Savannah. Christophe later became a leader in the struggle for Haitian independence from French colonial rule ending in 1804. A commander of the Haitian army, he became king of Haiti, the first head of state of African descent in the Western Hemisphere.

Acknowledging the deeds of "Les chasseurs volontaires de Saint Domingue" at Savannah, U.S. Secretary of State Cordell Hull dedicated a commemorative plaque on April 25, 1944, at the cathedral of Saint Marc, Haiti with these words:

"NOUS PAYONS AUJOURD'HUI TRIBUT AU COURAGE ET A L'ESPRIT DES VOLONTAIRES HAI-TIENS DE 1779 QUI RISQUERENT LEURS VIES POUR LA CAUSE DE LA LIBERTE DANS LES AMERIQUES.

"TODAY WE PAY TRIBUTE TO THE COURAGE AND SPIRIT OF THOSE HAITIAN VOLUNTEERS WHO IN 1779 RISKED THEIR LIVES FOR THE CAUSE OF AMERICAN LIBERTY."

Statements of significance

Military

The Siege of Savannah on Oct. 9, 1779 presents the American Revolution as a world conflict more than any other engagement of that war. The battle also reminds us that significant foreign resources of men, money, and material contributed to the eventual success of the cause of American independence. French, Polish, Native American, African slaves, free men of African descent, Germans, Hessians, Austrians, Scots, Welsh, Irish, English, Swedish, and American and West Indian colonials participated as individuals or whole units in this most culturally diverse battle of the war. For six weeks this diverse force was assembled in three armies to contend for the possession of Savannah. This battle resulted in the largest number of casualties the allies suffered in a single engagement.

The presence of the Chasseurs-Volontaires de Saint-Domingue as the largest unit of soldiers of African descent to fight in this war is worthy of commemoration. The fact that their number was made up of free men who volunteered for this expedition is startling to most people and surprising to many historians. Their presence reminds us that men of African heritage were to be found on most battlefields of the Revolution in large numbers. As a new and relatively inexperienced unit, the Chasseurs participated in the siege warfare including the battle of Sept. 24 and the siege of Oct. 9. Twenty-five themwere recorded as wounded or killed during the campaign. More than 60 were captured in the fall of Charleston eight month later. The British Navy captured three transports carrying Chasseurs, and these soldiers were made prizes of war and sold into slavery, Other members ot this unit were kept on duty away from their homes for many months as part of French garrison forces. A subsequent unit of Haitians participated in the French and Spanish campaign against Pensacola where they faced some of the same regiments of British troops that their comrades faced in Savannah.

The efforts of Haiti to secure its independence from colonial rule beginning in 1791 are remarkable for the fact that what began as a slave revolt ultimately prevailed over the resources of the French Empire and led to a government of Western Hemisphere Africans. Haiti, much smaller in population than the United States, was attacked by armies as large as those sent against America by Britain. The Haitian victory over the legions of Napoleon was achieved with much less foreign assistance than the United States enjoyed. Many key figures in the Haitian War of Independence gained military experience and political insights through their participation in Savannah -- most notably Henri Christophe, a youth at the time but later a general of Haitian armies and king of his nation for 14 years. There is little appreciation in the United
States for the events that led to the formation of the Haitian nation. Influenced by both the events of the American Revolution and the rhetoric of the French Revolution, the people of Haiti began a struggle for self-government and liberty. The first nation in the Western Hemisphere to form a government led by people of African descent, it also was the first nation to renounce slavery.

Politics/Government

The concepts of self-government and independence from European colonial rule were obvious elements in the siege of Savannah. To see these concepts tested on the battlefield was an experience that would be carried far afield from this and other Revolutionary War battlefields.

The figure of Henri Christophe as a young drummer participating in the campaign to take Savannah is an important figure in Haitian history. His rise from slave to king demonstrates a rare occurrence in human history. To rise from multigenerational bondage and to assume the role of soldier, officer, general, and then national leader and political architect is an almost unique human achievement. Henri Christophe accomplished this in the violent and turbulent times of the late 18th and early 19th centuries.

Mission of the Haitian American Historical Society (HAHS)

The Haitian American Historical Society (HAHS) is a 501(c) (3), non-profit organization with the support of numerous public officials at the local, state and federal level. The organization seeks to establish truth and accuracy in historical events pertaining to Haitians and those of Haitian descent. This allows current and future generations to understand and appreciate the role and contributions of Haitians to American society and other parts of the world. This is especially important for the next generation who could lose their identities and connection to Haiti.

Général George Biassou

George Biassou was one of the General of the slave revolt of 1791. He led the slave uprising to align with the pro-royalist Spanish authorities of Santo-Domingo April, 1792, the French legislature proclaimed the equality of all free people in the French colonies regardless of color, and sent a commission that was dominated by Léger-Félicité Sonthonax to Saint-Domingue to ensure that the colonial authorities complied. Biassou joined the Spaniard and went to Florida that was part of the Spanish Colony of Cuba. He was well established in St Augustine and was said to have the second highest pay in the Spanish Army. His rebellious years were over while the revolution he had started was raging in Haïti. He was the second highest paid official in St Augustine and lived with the honor and rank of a General. He died and is buried in Tolamato Cemetery St Augustine Florida.

Jean Baptiste Pointe Du Sable

Jean Baptiste Pointe du Sable (before 1745? St. Marc, Sainte-Domingue (now Haïti) - August 28, 1818, St. Charles, Mo.), popularly known as "The Father of Chicago", was a Haïtian colonist in North America of mixed French and African ancestry. Du Sable was simultaneously the first known nonindigenous settler and the firstAfrican-American/Afro-Caribbean in the area which is now Chicago, Illinois, in recognition whereof he was declared the Founder of Chicago by the State of Illinois and the City of Chicago on October 26, 1968.

Du Sable's birth year is highly uncertain, but is generally believed to have been between 1730 and 1745. Many of the stories about him are unconfirmed, especially those involving his early years. He was born at Saint-Marc in the French Caribbean colony of Saint-Domingue, present-day Haïti, to a slave named Suzanna and a French pirate's mate named Pointe du Sable who served on the Black Sea Gull. Suzanna may have been killed in a Spanish raid on Haïti. If this raid took place, Jean-Baptiste may have escaped by swimming out to his father's ship. After his father sent him to study at a Catholic school in France, du Sable and a friend, Jacques Clamorgan, traveled to Louisiana and then to Michigan, where he married a Potawatomi woman named Kittahawa (fleet-of-foot). To marry her, the twenty-five-year-old Jean Baptiste had to become a member of her tribe. He took an eagle as his tribal symbol. The Potawatomi called him "Black Chief," and he became a high-ranking member of the tribe. They had a son and daughter, Jean and Susanne.

In 1779, during the Revolutionary War, he was imprisoned briefly by the British in Fort Michilimackinac in Michigan, because of his French connections and on suspicion of being a US spy. He helped George Rogers Clark in his capture of Vincennes during the war. From the summer of 1780 until May of 1784, du Sable managed the Pinery, a huge tract of woodlands claimed by British Lt. Patrick Sinclair on the St. Clair River in eastern Michigan. Du Sable and his family lived at a cabin at the mouth of the Pine River in what is now the city of St. Clair.

Jean-Baptiste Pointe du Sable first arrived on the western shores of Lake Michigan about 1779, where he built the first permanent nonindigenous settlement, at the mouth of the river just east of the present Michigan Avenue Bridge on the north bank.

Before it was anything else, Chicago was a trading post. As its first permanent resident, du Sable operated the first fur-trading post during the two decades before his departure in 1800. Du Sable built his first house in the 1770s on the land now known as Pioneer Court, thirty years before Fort Dearborn was established on the banks of the Chicago River. By the time he sold out to John Kinzie's frontman, Jean La Lime, for 6,000 livres, his property included a house, two barns, horse-drawn mill, bakehouse, poultry house, dairy and a smokehouse. His home was a 22 by 40-foot (12 m) log cabin filled with fine furniture and paintings. In 1913, Milo M. Quaife, an historical librarian with the State Historical Society of Wisconsin, discovered the bill of sale from du Sable to Jean La Lime in an archive in Detroit. This document outlined all of the property du Sable owned as well as many of his personal artifacts.

In 1800, du Sable left Chicago for Peoria, Illinois, where he lived for a decade. Du Sable moved to St. Charles, Missouri in 1813, where his granddaughter lived. He died in 1818, the year Illinois became a state. He was buried in St. Charles, in an unmarked grave in St. Borromeo Cemetery. In 1968, the city erected a granite marker at du Sable's grave. The deed books in the office of the St. Charles County Recorder of Deeds do not support the assertions of some authors that du Sable sold land to Alexander McNair, who would become the first governor of Missouri.

The White House- press Office- Statement of President Barack Obama on Haitian Flag Day

The Briefing Room
The White House
Office of the Press Secretary

For Immediate Release   May 18, 2009

Statement of President Barack Obama on Haitian Flag Day

The United States and Haiti share a deeply intertwined history and a long standing friendship. In 1779, freemen from the French Colony of Saint Domingue, now the Republic of Haiti, came to the aid of American patriots fighting for the freedom at the Siege of Savannah. Today we remain connected by a Haitian-American community that contributes greatly to the economic, social, cultural, scientific and academic fabric of the United States and by my administration's steadfast commitment to come to the aid of those in Haiti working to ensure that Haiti's future is stable, Sustainable and prosperous. On this Haitian Flag Day, I am proud to send my warm wishes and those of the American People to the people of Haiti and the Haitian Diaspora as they celebrate during Haitian Heritage Month.

110TH CONGRESS
1ST SESSION

H. RES. 909

Commemorating the courage of the Haitian soldiers that fought for American independence in the "Siege of Savannah" and for Haiti's independence and renunciation of slavery.

IN THE HOUSE OF REPRESENTATIVES

DECEMBER 19, 2007

Mr. MEEK of Florida submitted the following resolution; which was referred to the Committee on Foreign Affairs

---

RESOLUTION

Commemorating the courage of the Haitian soldiers that fought for American independence in the "Siege of Savannah" and for Haiti's independence and renunciation of slavery.

Whereas in the fall of 1779, Haitian soldiers of the Chasseurs-Volontaires de Saint Domingue volunteered to join in the fight for American independence;

Whereas the unit was comprised of over 500 men of color from the island of Haiti;

Whereas on October 9, 1779, the soldiers of Chasseurs-Volontaires de Saint Domingue served as the largest unit of soldiers of African descent to fight in the "Siege of Savannah";

Whereas records show that over 500 men sailed treacherous waters to join the effort against the British;

Whereas over 300 of them lost their lives attempting to drive the British from Savannah;

Whereas the Savannah Monument, a project of the Haitian American Historical Society represents the Haitian soldiers that fought in the "Siege of Savannah";

Whereas the Savannah Monument was erected in Savannah, Georgia on Monday, October 8, 2007, to recognize the Haitian involvement in the fight for American independence; and

Whereas the Savannah Monument includes a statute of a 12-year-old drummer boy, depicting Mr. Henri Christophe, who became a leader in Haiti's Revolution to gain independence and renounce slavery: Now, therefore, be it

1   *Resolved,* That the House of Representatives com-
2 memorates the courage of the Haitian soldiers that fought
3 for American independence in the "Siege of Savannah"
4 and for Haiti's independence and renunciation of slavery.

○

State of Florida

HOUSE OF REPRESENTATIVES

House Resolution 9093

By Representative Brisé

A resolution honoring the Haitian soldiers of the Chasseurs-Volontaires de Saint-Domingue for their bravery and sacrifices in support of the United States of America during its War of Independence.

WHEREAS, in the fall of 1779, over 500 Haitian soldiers formed the Chasseurs-Volontaires de Saint-Domingue and joined other international forces supporting the United States in its fight for independence from British sovereignty, and

WHEREAS, the soldiers of the Chasseurs-Volontaires de Saint-Domingue served as the largest unit of soldiers of African descent to fight in the American War of Independence, and

WHEREAS, the soldiers of the Chasseurs-Volontaires de Saint-Domingue participated in the siege of Savannah, Georgia, which took six weeks and was one of the most culturally diverse battles of the War of Independence, fighting bravely in both the battle of September 24th and in the unsuccessful final siege of October 9th of 1779, and

WHEREAS, eight months later, over sixty members of the Chasseurs-Volontaires de Saint-Domingue were captured at the fall of Charleston, South Carolina, and

WHEREAS, many of the soldiers of the Chasseurs-Volontaires de Saint-Domingue lost their lives or their freedom attempting to help drive the British from the United States, and

WHEREAS, it is worthy of special commemoration that the Chasseurs-Volontaires de Saint-Domingue consisted entirely of free men who volunteered to fight against British sovereignty in support of the ideas of individual liberty and self-governance as embodied in the War of Independence, NOW, THEREFORE,

Be It Resolved by the House of Representatives of the State of Florida:

That the Haitian soldiers of the Chasseurs-Volontaires de Saint-Domingue are honored for their bravery and sacrifices in support of the United States of America during its War of Independence.

BE IT FURTHER RESOLVED that a copy of this resolution be presented to the Haitian American Historical Society and the Haitian Consulate in Florida as a tangible token of the sentiments expressed herein.

This is to certify the foregoing was adopted by publication in the Journal on April 9, 2008.

_____
Marco Rubio, Speaker

_____
William S. Pittman III, Chief Clerk

Glossary of terms

Arcahaie
Located north of the capital city of Port-au-Prince an hour's drive. It is the city where the Haitian flag was created.

Banana fritters
Deep fried mini-pancakes made with ripe banana.

Cap Haitian
The second largest city in Haiti and where the famous "Citadelle Laferiere" is built. It was also the Capital of King Christophe's kingdom.

Civadie
A beach famous for its beauty near Jacmel.

Creole
Language spoken by Haitians.

Griot
Favorite Haitian meal made of spicy pork meat fried in its own fat.

Hinche
City in the central part of Haiti and northeast of Port-au-Prince.

Jacmel
A city southeast of Port-au-Prince. Famous for its old houses and art works as well its gorgeous beaches.

Kenscoff
Vacation destination near Port-au-Prince

Labadie
Gorgeous beach near Cap Haitien and a favorite cruise ship destination.

Lambi
Sea conch, a favorite delicacy of Haitian cuisine.

Pain Patate
Sweet potato, banana and coconut pudding served with raisins.

Port-au-Prince
Capital city of Haiti